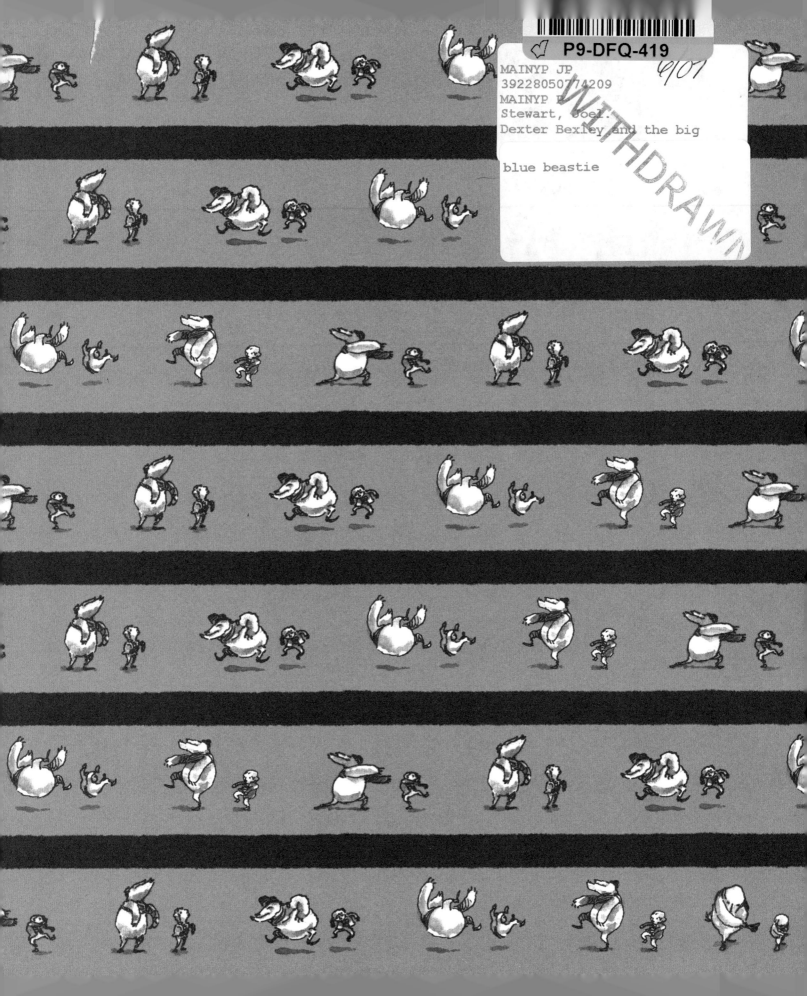

DEXTER BEXLEY
AND THE BIG
BLUE BEASTIE

In memory of Spook,
who knew when to go

First published in Great Britain in 2007 by Doubleday, an imprint of Random House Children's Books,

61-63 Uxbridge Road, London W5 5SA

First published in the United States of America by Holiday House, Inc. in 2007

Printed and Bound in Singapore

www.holidayhouse.com

First Edition

1 3 5 7 9 10 8 6 4 2

Library of Congress Cataloging-in-Publication Data

Stewart, Joel.

Dexter Bexley and the big blue beastie / by Joel Stewart. — 1st ed.

p. cm.

Summary: After running into a big blue beastie with his scooter,

Dexter tries to come up with increasingly inventive ideas

to keep the beastie from eating him.

ISBN-13: 978-0-8234-2068-1 (hardcover)

[1. Imagination—Fiction. 2. Play—Fiction.

3. Monsters—Fiction. 4. Friendship—Fiction.]

I. Title.

PZ7.S84928Dex 2007

[E]—dc22

2006043698

DEXTER BEXLEY
AND THE BIG
BLUE BEASTIE

JOEL STEWART

HOLIDAY HOUSE / New York

Dexter Bexley scooted . . .

. . . and scooted.

Right into . . .

. . . a Big Blue Beastie!

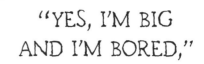

But Dexter Bexley had a much better idea.

"HOLD ON.
I HAVE A
MUCH BETTER IDEA,"

said Dexter Bexley.

Dexter Bexley and the Big Blue Beastie scooted . . .

Dexter Bexley and the Big Blue Beastie

went into business

delivering flowers.

Dexter Bexley and the Big Blue Beastie gave up
the flower delivery business and became . . .

BEXLEY AND BEAST:
Private Detectives.

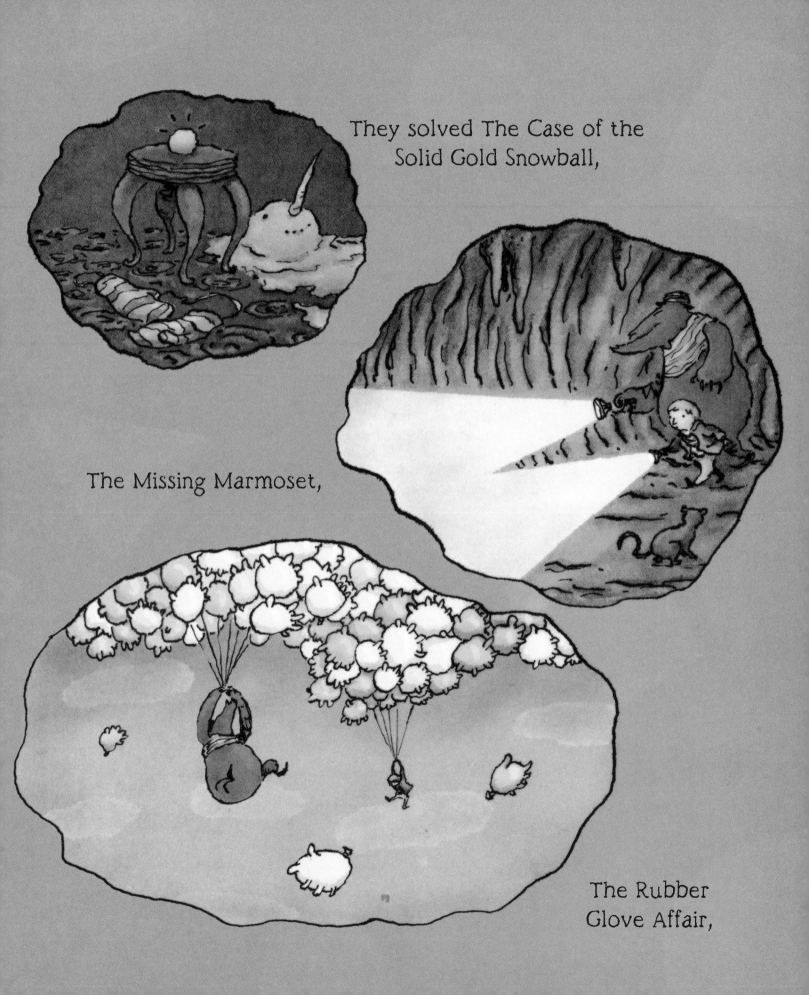

They solved The Case of the
Solid Gold Snowball,

The Missing Marmoset,

The Rubber
Glove Affair,

The Bicycle from Beyond,

and The Great Sausage Heist.

They even apprehended their archnemesis, Professor Hortern Zoar,

though he later escaped.

"I'M HUNGRY,"

said the Big Blue Beastie.

"HOLD ON!"

Dexter Bexley invented the biggest, stickiest, tastiest Yogurt, Fudge, Banana, Ice-creamy Beastie Feast ever!

Really, it was huge!

But for once Dexter Bexley
was clean out of ideas.

"I'M CLEAN OUT OF IDEAS,"

said Dexter Bexley.

"I SUPPOSE NOW
YOU'LL **HAVE** TO EAT ME UP."

The Big Blue Beastie bought himself
a very gooey lollipop.

And one for Dexter Bexley.

. . . NOW THAT I'VE FOUND A FRIEND."

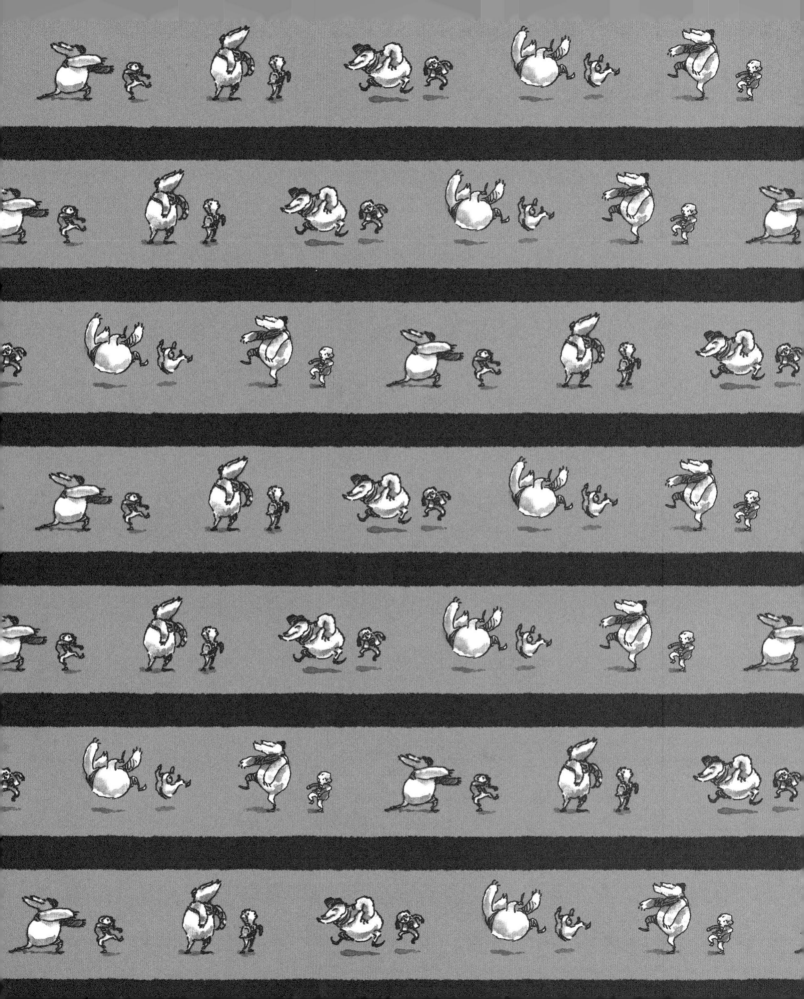